You are about to enter the

Wonderful World of

Alfie
Green

On his ninth birthday Alfie Green got a very special present – a magical book left by his grandad.

The book gives Alfie special powers and opens a whole new wonderful world ....

JOE O'BRIEN is an award-winning gardener who lives in Ballyfermot in Dublin. This is his second book about the wonderful world of Alfie Green.

DEDICATION

The *Alfie Green* series is dedicated to my son, Ethan, who in his short time in this world taught me to be strong, happy and thankful for the gift of life. Thank you, Ethan, for the inspiration to write.

Alfie Green and A Sink Full of Frogs is dedicated to my son, Jamie, who makes every day the best day.

ACKNOWLEDGEMENTS

Thanks, firstly and especially, to Linda Kenny for your encouragement, your help in making this happen and your friendship. To Mary O'Sullivan, Patricia Crowley. To Mary Webb, Ide ní Laoghaire, Emma Byrne and all at O'Brien Press for their great work. Jean Texier for the wonderful illustrations. A special thanks to Michael O'Brien, the publisher.
To my late mum, who introduced me to the joys of gardening. My dad. My late and dear friend, Paddy Kelly. Finally, very special thanks to my wife and best friend Mandy.

*　　　*　　　*

JEAN TEXIER is a storyboard artist and illustrator. Initially trained in animation, he has worked in the film industry for many years.

Alfie
and a SINK FULL of FROGS
Green

Joe O'Brien

Illustrated by JeanTexier

THE O'BRIEN PRESS
DUBLIN

This paperback edition first published 2007 by The O'Brien Press Ltd.,
12 Terenure Road East, Rathgar, Dublin 6, Ireland.
Tel: +353 1 4923333; Fax: +353 1 4922777
E-mail: books@obrien.ie
Website: www.obrien.ie
First published 2005 in hardback by The O'Brien Press Ltd

ISBN: 978-1-84717-079-8

British Library Cataloguing-in-Publication Data
A catalogue reference for this title is available from the British
Library

2 3 4 5 6 7 8 9 10
07 08 09 10 11

The O'Brien Press receives
assistance from

Editing, typesetting, layout, design: The O'Brien Press Ltd.
Illustrations: Jean Texier
Printed and bound in the UK by J.H. Haynes & Co Ltd, Sparkford

CONTENTS

CHAPTER 1

Bugs!

'Ouch!' yelled Alfie Green, sucking
his thumb where a thorn had just
pricked it.

'Ow!'
said the
rose bush,
as a
greenfly
took a big
bite out of
his leaf.

'Quick, Alfie, squash it.'

Alfie had been so busy with school and homework that he hadn't noticed all the bugs in his garden. Now he was squishing greenflies as quickly as his fingers could move, and still there were more of them.

'What on earth is Alfie up to?' asked Mrs Butler from next door.

Mrs Butler was enjoying a nice cup of tea and a big slice of homemade ginger cake with Alfie's mother and his granny.

'Is he talking to himself?'

Alfie's granny laughed, which is not a good idea when your mouth is full of ginger cake.

A crumb caught in her throat and she had to be hit on the back a few times, coughing and spluttering until she could speak again.

'Alfie isn't talking to himself,' she explained. 'He's talking to the plants, just like his grandad did when he was alive.'

'Oh, I see,' said Mrs Butler, although she didn't really.

'Well, it's time for me to go home,'
she said. 'Thank you for the tea.'

She got up, and then sat down
again suddenly. 'Oh dear, my leg has
gone to sleep.'

'Alfie!' his mother called.

Alfie ran in from the garden. His fingers were covered in greenfly mush.

'What is it, Mam?'

'Mrs Butler's leg is gone to sleep. Lend her a hand back to her house.'

'Wouldn't I be better lending her a leg?'asked Alfie.

'Don't be so smart,' said his mother, but she was smiling.

CHAPTER 2

THE SINK IN THE HEDGE

Alfie helped Mrs Butler into her house. She poured him a glass of lemonade and he drank it so quickly that the bubbles fizzed in his nose and made him sneeze.

'While you're here, Alfie, would you mind bringing in the washing from the line?' Mrs Butler asked.

'No problem,' Alfie said, and grabbed the laundry basket by the door.

He had taken only a few steps into the garden when he heard a voice.

'Great,' it said. 'It's the young lad from next door. Here, you!'

Alfie walked over to the privet hedge.

'What's the matter?'

'Is there any chance you could give me a bit of a trim?' the hedge asked. 'I'm feeling very ragged.'

'You could do with a bit off the top,' Alfie agreed. 'As soon as I've brought in the washing, I'll get my shears.'

Mrs Butler had fallen asleep in front of the television. She was having a strange dream of gingerbread dogs chasing sneezing cats when Alfie woke her.

She jumped in her chair.

'Will I cut your hedge for you, Mrs Butler?' Alfie asked.

'That would be lovely,' said Mrs
Butler and fell asleep again.

It wasn't long before the hedge
looked very smart. Alfie was picking
up the clippings when he saw
something white hidden underneath
the hedge.

'What's that?' he asked.

'That old thing?' said the hedge.
'That's a sink that was thrown out
years ago and forgotten. I wish
someone would take it away. I nearly
fall over it every time I stretch my
legs.'

CHAPTER 3

PEEP! PEEP!

Mrs Butler was glad to get rid of the sink.

There was only one problem – it was too heavy for Alfie to lift on his own.

He waited until his dad and his brother Dermot got back from football training in the park.

Then the three of them dragged the sink out of the hedge and across the lawn.

As they went out through the gate, Alfie heard the hedge give a big **'Aaaaaahhhhhh'**, like his dad did when he took off his shoes after work and wriggled his toes by the fireplace.

'Put it just there,' said Alfie. 'No, there. No, maybe here. Or maybe over–'

'Alfie!' said his dad crossly. 'Make up your mind! My back is killing me.'

Alfie's dad had gone red in the face.

'Alright,' Alfie decided finally, 'Right there, by the fuchsia bush.'

'The *what* bush?' Mr Green knew nothing about gardening.

'Fuchsia, F-E-W-S-H-A, that bush with the red flowers that look like umbrellas.'

'Oh, right.'

'Thanks, Dad,' Alfie said, and Mr Green escaped into the house before Alfie could change his mind again.

That night Alfie fell asleep thinking of all the things he could plant in his sink.

He was so tired from bug-**Squishing**, hedge-**Clipping** and bringing in washing that he didn't wake up even when it began to rain and huge drops fell on the roof like hundreds of exploding water-bombs.

Early next morning Alfie headed out to the sink. Oh no! It was full of water. He should have taken the stopper out. He pushed his sleeves right up and reached into the cold water.

Up from the water peeped lots of little eyes, then little heads.

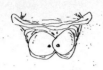

Frogs!

Alfie didn't want frogs in his sink.

He didn't want frogs in his garden.

What was he going to do?

Maybe the wise old plant in the

magical book could help?

CHAPTER 4

THE WISE OLD PLANT

Alfie ran to the garden shed and moved the loose floorboard. He took out the old box, turned the key in the lock and lifted out the magical book.

He opened the book and placed his hand on the seed on the first page.

The seed began to spin and spin and then the wise old plant rose up from the page, its crinkly leaves unfolding and sprouting long, pointy blue hairs.

'What can I do for you, Alfie?' asked the plant.

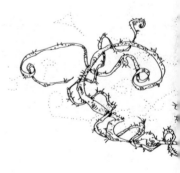

Alfie said, all in in rush, 'Mrs Butler gave me a sink and I was going to plant it and I put the stopper in and then it rained and it filled up with water and now it's full of frogs and what will I do to get rid of them and–'

'**Stop! Stop!**' said the wise old plant. 'You're wilting my leaves.'

He shook himself and straightened out a few leaves that had started to droop.

'Alfie,' he said. 'Don't you know how *lucky* you are to have frogs?'

'Lucky?' asked Alfie.

'Yes, very lucky.' The wise old plant leaned down and began to flick over the pages of the magical book.

He stopped when he reached the page that said 'A Sink Full of Frogs'.

A garden appeared on the page – Alfie's garden.

There were frogs in Alfie's garden, lots of frogs. They were leaping from one place to another, chasing insects and eating slugs and snails until their little green bellies were stuffed to bursting.

Alfie was amazed.

'Wow! I didn't know that frogs ate insects and slugs and all the things that hurt my plants.'

The wise old plant nodded and then folded itself back into the book, which closed with a

Alfie hurried back into the house.

'You'll be late for school,' his mother scolded. 'Were you out in the garden emptying the sink?'

Alfie stuffed a slice of burnt toast and marmalade into his mouth and crunched the pieces between his teeth.

'No, Mam,' he said. 'I'm NEVER going to empty the sink.'

CHAPTER 5

A MAGIC SWIMMING POOL

Alfie hopped and skipped his way to school, as if he had turned into one of his new little green friends.

The frogs were happy too. They bounced around Alfie's garden all morning, chasing insects.

Then disaster struck!

One of the frogs landed too heavily on the leaf of a hosta plant and broke it.

'You slimy slug-sucker!' shouted the hosta.

'I'm very sorry,' said the little frog. She looked as if she was going to cry.

'Don't upset the frogs,' an older hosta whispered. 'We need them to eat the slugs and snails.'

He turned to the sad frog and said, 'Take no notice of him. Why don't you go for a nice swim in the magic swimming pool beside the fuchsia bush?

'Did you know that the water in that pool will make you jump higher and further than all the other frogs?'

A magic swimming pool! The frog cheered up immediately and hopped off to tell all her friends.

CHAPTER 6

FROGS EVERYWHERE!

As soon as school was over, Alfie rushed home. As he turned the corner near his house he saw something that made him drop his schoolbag like a ton of bricks.

There were frogs in the hedges, on the walls, on the bonnets of cars. A queue of frogs stretched from Mr Skully's house, four doors down, through Alfie's gate and up the path to his front door.

There were frogs **EVERYWHERE!**

Alfie's granny was sitting on the banisters, yelling: 'They're in my bath. They're everywhere; get them off me!'

Alfie ran around to the back garden. Lucy was sitting by the patio doors with her rabbits, Posh and Becks, in her arms.

'You're in big trouble, Alfie Green,' she said.

'My garden!' Alfie cried in horror. There were so many frogs that it looked like the grass was moving.

'Never mind your stupid garden!' Lucy said crossly. 'Poor Posh and

Becks are terrified. The frogs are diving off their hutch into the sink. You'd think it was the Olympics!'

Alfie heard a voice calling to him from the border. It was the hosta with the broken leaf.

Alfie tread carefully across the grass, trying not to splatter any frogs.

'What is it?' asked Alfie.

'I think this might be *our* fault,' admitted the hosta.

He told Alfie the whole story. It seemed that the frogs had spread the news about the 'magic' swimming pool to all their aunts and uncles and cousins and friends. And now they were all here!

'Well, you won't have to worry about snails and slugs anymore,' said Alfie crossly.

'Why?' asked the hosta.

'Because when this mess is fixed, you're going on the compost heap!'

CHAPTER 7

THE DANCING FIDDLER

Alfie ran into the shed and lifted the floorboard. He told the wise old plant what had happened.

'What a mess!' said the plant. 'You're going to need some help. I'd better **hop** to it!'

His leaves shook with laughter as he flicked through the pages of the ancient book.

'Ah, this is what I was looking for,' he said at last, pointing to a page that said, 'The Dancing Fiddler'. 'Now, watch carefully.'

A picture of a village appeared on the page. There were frogs – hundreds of them – hopping through the streets and getting under everybody's feet. Then, out from behind a tree came a very small man with a fiddle under his chin. He raised the bow and began to play. And all at once the frogs stopped hopping. They began to dance.

'Why are they dancing?' Alfie was amazed.

'The dancing fiddler is playing a tune,' said the wise old plant. 'Listen.'

Faintly at first, and then louder came the sound of the merriest, happiest music Alfie had ever heard in his life. His feet started to tap and his head bobbed up and down.

As the fiddler played, the frogs danced along behind him. When he turned, they turned, where he went, they went.

The villagers cheered as the frogs followed the fiddler along the road and across the fields.

They disappeared into the distance as if nothing else in the world mattered but the sound of the fiddle.

'Wow!' said Alfie. 'That's just what I need. But where would I get a dancing fiddler?'

The wise old plant looked at Alfie. 'I can't do *everything*, Alfie. You must find the fiddler yourself, then I'll see what I can do.'

And with that, the wise old plant folded himself back into the magical book, which closed with a

CHAPTER 8

A BRILLIANT IDEA

Alfie thought and thought, and finally he had an idea. He hurried across the road to where his best friend, Fitzer, lived.

Fitzer's mother was standing on her wall, swiping at frogs with her sweeping brush.

She looked very cross.

Fitzer shouted down from his bedroom window. 'Alfie, you nutter! What have you done?

The two pals sat on the footpath.

'I have a plan,' said Alfie. 'You know Old Podge down the road? I'm going to ask him for help.'

'Podge Kelly? Are you mad?' asked Fitzer. 'He's a sandwich short of a picnic!'

'Maybe,' said Alfie. 'But he plays the fiddle, doesn't he?'

'What's that got to do with anything?' Fitzer was confused.

'I need to turn him into a dancing fiddler to get rid of the frogs,' explained Alfie.

For a minute Fitzer looked worried. Had Alfie lost it completely?

Then his face lit up.

'Like the Pied Piper, you mean?'

'Yes,' Alfie agreed. 'Something like that.'

Alfie and Fitzer knocked hard on Podge's door.

'Go away,' shouted the old man. 'I'm not selling my house; I don't want to buy anything and I didn't order pizza!'

'We're not selling anything, Mr Kelly. It's Alfie Green and Dean Fitzpatrick,' Alfie shouted through the letterbox.

Podge had been a gardening friend of Alfie's grandad's, although Podge only grew vegetables.

The door creaked open and he let the boys in.

CHAPTER 9

A HERO?

Alfie told Podge about his problem with the frogs and how the only way to get rid of them was with a dancing fiddler.

'Me! A dancing fiddler!' Podge exclaimed. 'No, no. I'm much too old for that sort of thing.'

'But you'd be a hero, Mr Kelly,' Alfie said.

A hero! That sounded good to Podge, and it was a very long time

since anyone had thought he could be
useful for anything.

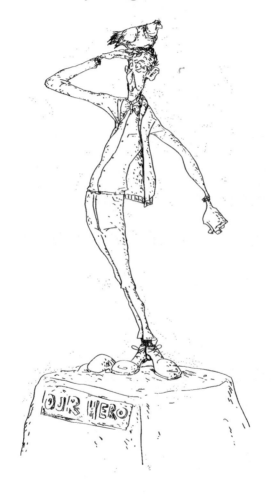

'I'll do it!' he agreed. 'But what will I do with all the frogs?'

Alfie had that worked out, too.

'Well, if they were in your garden, you wouldn't have any trouble with slugs and snails again. Imagine the size your vegetables would grow to? Record-breaking, I reckon.'

A hero, and with record-breaking vegetables? Old Podge liked the sound of that.

He had been trying to win the **BIGGEST CABBAGE** prize at the local gardening competition for years and

years, but Jimmy Skully always beat
him.

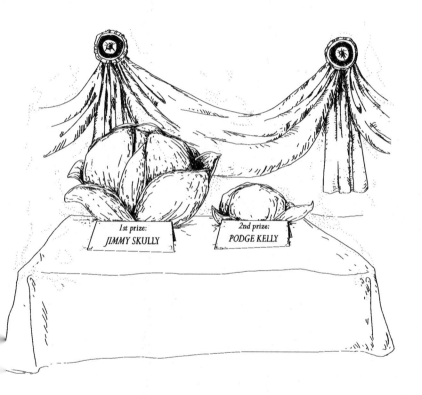

'Okay, Alfie. Sounds good to me.'

'Now,' said Alfie, remembering how the fiddler in the picture had looked. 'We need to make a few small changes.'

He noticed that Podge's curtains were made of green velvet. Alfie and Fitzer took down one of the curtains and tied it to the old man's shoulders with a safety pin and an **80 TODAY** birthday badge that was stuck in a cushion on the armchair.

Podge rolled his black socks up over his trousers, stuck his pipe in his mouth, popped an old cap on his

head and tucked his fiddle under his
chin.

'Wow!' said Alfie. 'You look great. Just like a real dancing fiddler.'

Old Podge was chuffed.

'Right, time to round up the frogs,' he said, heading for the door.

CHAPTER 10

THE GREAT FROG ROUND-UP

They began in Alfie's garden.

'Now,' said Podge, 'what tune will I play?'

'Oh ... eh ...' Alfie sent a silent HELP to the wise old plant, and immediately a shower of tiny blue glittery dust hovered over the old man and settled on his fiddle.

'Play anything you like, Mr Kelly.'
Alfie said.

Podge began to play. Out of his
fiddle came the very same merry
dancing tune that Alfie had heard
from the magical book.

The frogs stopped what they were doing and began to sway.

Podge played his way past the sink, around the garden and out through the gate. Every now and then he gave a little skip or shook his leg like a real Irish dancer.

The frogs followed, dancing in a long line, more and more joining in as Podge led them down the road.

'Hurray! It's working,' Alfie and Fitzer cheered.

Frogs came from all directions. They leapt from cars and hedges; they

jumped fences as if they were horses
in the Grand National.

The neighbours came out of their houses to see what was going on.

'My goodness! Is that Mr Kelly?' asked Fitzer's mother as she climbed down from the wall.

'Mrs Green, come quickly,' she shouted across the road to Alfie's granny. 'Look at Mr Kelly dancing.'

Alfie's granny came to the gate. Hmm, she thought, I wonder if Mr Kelly would come dancing with me?

She began to clap. Mrs Fitzpatrick
joined in and soon all the neighbours

were cheering Podge as he made his
way towards his house.

In no time at all, the frogs were
safely in Podge's garden, still dancing.

Podge led them to his vegetable
patch and when the music stopped
they began munching away at the
slugs they found.

Alfie made sure to empty out his
sink that very afternoon. He filled it

with earth and then planted lots of Alpine plants. There would be no more magic swimming pool!

After a few days, most of the frogs had gone back to the ponds and streams and ditches where they lived.

Podge kept just enough to make sure his vegetables were slug-free, and rewarded the busy frogs with a tune and a dance every morning.

His vegetables were so happy and healthy that they grew to twice the size of Jimmy Skully's!

And it was all thanks to Alfie
Green and his magical gift.

READ ALFIE'S OTHER GREAT ADVENTURES IN:

Alfie Green and the Magical Gift

A rusty key opens a dusty box hidden in Alfie's grandad's shed. Inside is an old, old book — with magical powers. The book promises Alfie a gift, but first he must take the crystal flower across Sleepy Meadows full of Snapping Dragons to the crooked tree that is guarded by Giant Hogweeds. If Alfie succeeds he will be able to do something he has never done before!

Alfie Green and the Bee-Bottle Gang

Alfie is in big trouble.

He stopped Whacker Walsh and his gang from trapping bees in the park and now they are out to get him. What can he do?

The wise old plant in the magical book comes up with a plan that sends Alfie back to Arcania in search of the Queen Bee in Honeycomb Mountain.

Alfie needs back-up — and he needs it NOW!

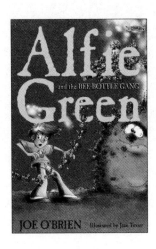

Alfie Green and the Fly-Trapper

Alfie's house is invaded by flies. His fly-trap plant is too small to eat them all so the wise old plant uses magic to make it bigger.

Then it gets BIGGER and BIGGER and BIGGER. Nothing is safe! Alfie decides the only place for the Giant Fly Trapper is in the Belching Bogs in Arcania.

But to get there he must outwit the creatures of the Nanabur Mines and the deadly worm monster.

Alfie Green and the Monkey Puzzler

The circus has come to town. But it's no ordinary circus, it's Monty's Marvellous Monkey Circus and all the performers are monkeys!

All the kids from Budsville are really excited, except for Alfie who suspects all is not what it seems ...

Alfie Green and the Conker King

Alfie would love to win the School Conker Championship.

But with Conor Hoolihan on his team and Whacker Walsh cheating all the time, he has no chance. He needs to find a Super Cracking Conker, fast.

Alfie journeys to the Skeleton Woods of Arcania to find the last great king of the conker warriors.

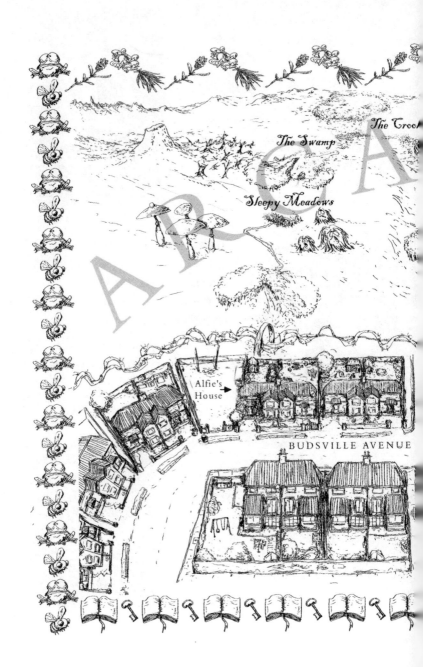

The Creek

The Swamp

Sleepy Meadows

Alfie's House →

BUDSVILLE AVENUE

The
Wonderful World of
Alfie Green

SYCAMORE ROAD

LAUREL PARK

BUDSVILLE PRIMARY SCHOOL